THE SEASONS AND SOMEONE

HARCOURT BRACE & COMPANY

San Diego   New York   London

THE SEASONS AND SOMEONE

WRITTEN BY

Virginia Kroll

ILLUSTRATED BY

Tatsuro Kiuchi

To my best friend,
Barbara Wilson Halvorsen,
and our wonderful Juan-Tin River
——VIRGINIA KROLL

To Sadao and Fusae
——TATSURO KIUCHI

Text copyright © 1994 by Virginia Kroll
Illustrations copyright © 1994 by Tatsuro Kiuchi

Requests for permission to make copies
of any part of the work should be mailed to:
Permissions Department, Harcourt Brace & Company,
6277 Sea Harbor Drive,
Orlando, Florida 32887-6777.

Kroll, Virginia L.
The seasons and Someone/Virginia Kroll;
illustrated by Tatsuro Kiuchi.
p. cm.
Summary: A young Eskimo girl witnesses
the changing seasons in Alaska.
ISBN 0-15-271233-X
1. Eskimos—Juvenile fiction. [1. Eskimos—Fiction.
2. Indians of North America—Fiction. 3. Seasons—Fiction.]
I. Kiuchi, Tatsuro, ill. II. Title.
K9227Se 1994
[E]—dc20   93-11123

Printed in Singapore
First edition   A B C D E

The paintings in this book were done in oil on
Crescent illustration board no. 310.
The display type was set in Neuland Inline by
Harcourt Brace & Company Photocomposition
Center, San Diego, California.
The text type was set in Deepdene by
Harcourt Brace & Company Photocomposition
Center, San Diego, California.
Color separations were made by Bright Arts, Ltd., Singapore.
Printed and bound by Tien Wah Press, Singapore
This book was printed with soya-based inks on Leykam recycled
paper, which contains more than 20 percent postconsumer waste
and has a total recycled content of at least 50 percent.
Production supervision by Warren Wallerstein and Ginger Boyer
Designed by Trina Stahl and Michael Farmer

AUTHOR'S NOTE

ESKIMOS INHABIT THE northernmost areas of the world: Alaska, Greenland, and parts of Canada and Asia. Their remarkable ingenuity enables them to survive the bleakest, most bitter climate. They have a deep appreciation for the land, animals, and natural resources, and their culture is rich with many fascinating customs.

According to an ancient Eskimo belief, it is bad luck for a person to speak his or her own name aloud, so the person uses the pronoun "Someone" or "Somebody" instead. Some Eskimos still practice this and other traditions, and many mix modern ways with old.

The Bearded Ones in this story are the hardy musk-oxen, shaggy bovine beasts with huge, curved horns.

An igloo is an Eskimo house, no matter what material is used to construct it, although many people use the word to mean only the coned ice-house made of snow blocks, a temporary winter home. Skins are used to make temporary summer dwellings, and sod, wood, or stone are used for permanent homes.

WHAT WILL HAPPEN when the field turns gold turns brown turns sparkling white? Hare, Ptarmigan, Lemming, Fox, and Ermine will wear new coats and whisk through winter like filmy ghosts.

The Bearded Ones will trudge up to the lonely ridges. Snowball fringe will trim their skirts as they nibble frosted willows.

Wolf will howl hunger.

And Someone will savor the last few berries in the basket, bittersweet and full of seeds.

What will happen when Sun disappears for months, leaving Moon in her daytime place?

Whale oil and summer moss will burn in the soapstone candle.
Fish stew steam will curl around the kitchen.
A fire of driftwood and brittle sticks will show the new lines on
Papa's face and in Mama's weathered hands.

And Someone will rinse and wrap the berry seeds in paper and tuck them away in a safe, dry place.

What will happen when Blizzard swallows the village and Wind pounds at the igloo door?

Grandmother will chew leather until it is soft, and Mama will sew it into sealskin boots, as the elders did long ago.

Papa will carve a doll of bone, and Brother will make a soapstone whale.

And Someone, snuggled in a shaggy wool shawl, will hunger for the taste of plump red berries.

What will happen when Wind's roars change to whispers and icicles grow thin?

Lichen will dapple rocks, imitating snowflakes.

Ground Squirrel will scurry from her burrow.

Ptarmigan's feathers will blend with brown brush again.

Fox and Lemming will try to outrun each other.

And Someone will laugh aloud to see buds on the berry bushes.

What will happen when bushes burst into clouds of green?
The ground will thunder with returning caribou.
Flocks of geese will flow like black ribbons, winding and looping
across the sky.

The Bearded Ones will rub against rocks to rid themselves of wool.
Someone will collect their tufts for next winter's shawl and then run
to the igloo panting, "Mama! Papa! The berries are blossoming!"

What will happen when Sun grows tired of hiding and tells Moon to stay away?

Ermine, Lemming, Fox, and Hare will change their coats to match the soil.

Villagers will scoop seaweed and silver fishes with their fingers from
flooding streams.

And Someone will touch the tiny green balls and sigh, "Someone
can't wait."

What will happen when sweet, short Summer explodes in
splashes of scarlet, purple, pink, and blue?
  Butterfly will unfurl her wings.
  The air will fill with buzzing bees and murmuring mosquitoes.
  Walrus will belly flop in the unfrozen sea, then lumber onto shore
to sunbathe with Seal.
  Cabbages will grow wider than a child is tall.

And Someone, with wildly waving arms, will shoo the birds away
from the ripening berries.

What will happen when gulls gather on the cliffs?
Duck and Dovekie will quack and squabble.
Snow Bunting, Snowy Owl, and Swan will add their voices to the
chorus, and Ocean will hush, for a moment, to listen.
Polar Bear will pant, wishing for Winter.

Little Sister will cup her hands around Eiderduck's egg and suck its creamy liquid.

And Someone's hands will turn red from picking basketfuls of berries.

What will happen when Someone makes dessert of berries and whipped blubber?

The family will lick their lips and scrape every drop from their bowls.

Someone will go outside after supper and feel breezes ruffling straight black hair.

Someone will give thanks for The Beautiful Land, then unwrap last winter's seeds and drop them into the soil next to the old berry bushes.

Someone, with closed, dreaming eyes, will imagine the new sprouts of springtime.

And the souls of ancestors and animals will smile all around.